W9-CTX-881

Birthday
Book Club Donation
by

Blake feece

2005

CARS

Nancy Smiler Levinson

illustrated by
Jacqueline Rogers

Holiday House / New York

For their assistance and expertise in the preparation of this book,
the author thanks Summer Kay, Education and Museum Services
Manager, National Automobile Museum (The Harrah Collection),
Reno, Nevada; and Peter Gariepy, Senior Judge,
Antique Automobile Club of America.

With special thanks from the illustrator to Summer Kay
and the National Automobile Museum, Tom Meyn,
Dwight Sawyer, and Suzanne Reinoehl.

Library of Congress Cataloging-in-Publication Data
Levinson, Nancy Smiler.
Cars / written by Nancy Smiler Levinson; illustrated by Jacqueline Rogers.
p. cm.
Summary: Briefly describes the early development of automobiles
and their impact on daily life.
ISBN 0-8234-1614-3 (hardcover)
1. Automobiles—History—Juvenile literature.
[1. Automobiles—History.] I. Rogers, Jacqueline, ill. II. Title.
TL147.L45 2004
629.222'09—dc21
2003050922

To my mother, Minnie Smiler,
who remembers the thrill of riding
in her father's new motorcar long ago
N. S. L.

To Justin D.
J. R.

First Renault, 1899

Long ago,
if people wanted to go far,
they took a boat or train.
Most people rode on horseback.
Horses pulled carriages.

They also pulled fire
and ambulance wagons.
Horses got tired pulling heavy loads.
They needed care and feeding
all the time.

Many people asked,

"Can a carriage move

without a horse?"

The first horseless carriages

ran on steam.

They looked like

big teakettles on wheels.

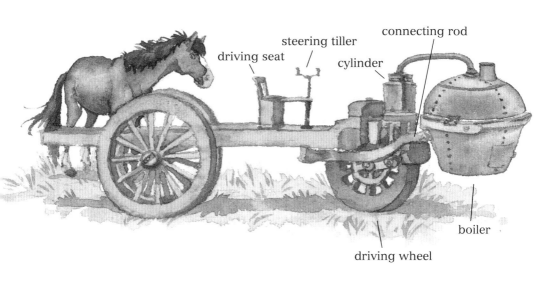

connecting rod

steering tiller

driving seat

cylinder

boiler

driving wheel

They were loud and smoky.
To start a "steamer,"
a driver put water in the boiler.
He had to wait a half hour
for it to boil.

Other horseless carriages
ran on electricity.
The electricity came from batteries.
They could not go far.
A driver had to stop
and recharge the battery.

In 1886 two men in Germany
built the first gas-powered engines.
Karl Benz put an engine
on a big tricycle.
He tried it out in his yard.
Once he took his wife for a drive.
They hit a brick wall.
But no one was hurt.

Gottlieb Daimler fitted an engine
in a stagecoach.
It was the first
motorcar with four wheels.

In 1893 two brothers built
the first gasoline-powered motorcar
in the United States. They were
Frank and Charles Duryea
of Springfield, Massachusetts.

On Thanksgiving Day, 1895,
Frank drove in a race in Chicago.
He raced with five other drivers.
They drove fifty-two miles
in cold and snow.

They stopped to fix their cars
along the way.
Frank finished the race in first place.
It took him ten hours
and twenty-three minutes.

In 1896 Henry Ford made
his first motorcar.
He used four bicycle wheels,
a bench seat, and a tiller to steer.
He used bits of metal
and a pipe
to make an engine.
He tried out the engine
in his kitchen sink.

In 1903 Ford opened a factory
in Detroit, Michigan.
His workers could build
many cars at one time.

Ford's Model T was easy to drive.
It was cheap to buy.
People called it the Tin Lizzie.
It became the most popular
car of its time.

Before a Sunday drive,

a family had to buy a can of gasoline

in a store.

There were no gas stations.

Their new motorcar

had no roof or windshield.

They bumped along a dirt road.

Dust flew behind the tires.

Mama wore a long coat, goggles,
and a beehive bonnet.
Papa wore a cap with earmuffs,
goggles, and gloves.
The children wore hoods.
So did their pet dog!

Suddenly the motorcar skidded
off the road into the mud!
A farmer and his horse
came by.
The horse pulled the car out
of the mud.
At last the family was driving again.
It was a good day after all!

Not all people liked motorcars.
"They will never take the place
of horses," one newspaper said.
Many people thought cars
were dangerous.
A law was passed in England:
A man had to walk in front
of every motorcar.
He waved a red flag or lantern
to warn people close by.

Horses were afraid of cars, too.
In Michigan a man made a wooden
horse head.
He put it on the front of his car.
He thought it would make
horses less afraid.
But it did not work.

Every year cars were improved.
Gasoline stations and
repair shops were built.
Roads were paved.
Road signs and maps were printed.
City and farm families visited
one another more often.
Farmers used trucks to bring
food to many markets.

Families got fresher food to eat.
More country children
went to school.
Doctors helped sick people
who lived far from hospitals.
Cars changed life
for people all over the world.

Today cars fill
the streets and highways.
They use more and more gasoline.
Too much gasoline harms the air.
Engineers are trying out new cars
to help fix the growing problem.

One is the hybrid car.
It is powered
by battery *and* gas.
Someday new kinds of fuel
will replace gasoline.
Cars will be better for all of us.

TIME LINE

1770

Nicolas Cugnot of France introduced
a three-wheel horseless carriage powered
by a steam engine.

1830s–1920s

Battery-powered electric engines were built
in Scotland, England, France, Belgium,
Holland, and the United States.

1886

In Germany, Karl Benz built the first successful
gasoline-powered engine. Gottlieb Daimler
built a gasoline-powered four-wheel carriage.

from left to right: 1770 Cugnot steam engine, 1893 Duryea gas
buggy, 1896 Ford quadricycle, 1912 Baker electric brougham

from left to right: 1929 Ford Roadster, 1938 Buick "Y,"
1967 Volkswagen Beetle, 2003 Honda Insight (hybrid)

1893

The Duryea brothers produced

the first gasoline-powered motorcar

in the United States.

1896

Henry Ford built his first motorcar.

1897

Ransom E. Olds built his first motorcar

in Lansing, Michigan.

1903

Ford founded the Ford Motor Company.

1908

Ford introduced the Model T.

GLOSSARY

battery A box for storing energy that can be changed into electricity.

boiler A tank that heats water to make steam.

carriage A vehicle on wheels pulled by a horse or moved by an engine. The word *car* comes from *carriage*.

cylinder A tube in an engine that holds metal plugs. The plugs move up and down to help the wheels turn.

electric engine A motor that runs on a battery.

gasoline engine A motor that runs on gasoline.

Model T The name Henry Ford gave to one

of his first cars. Others were Models A, B, C, F, K, M, N, R, and S.

recharge To give a battery energy again.

stagecoach A horse-drawn carriage carrying passengers and mail.

steam engine A motor that turns hot water into steam to run a car.

steamer A steam-powered carriage.

tiller A rod or stick used for steering.

DIFFERENT ENGINES

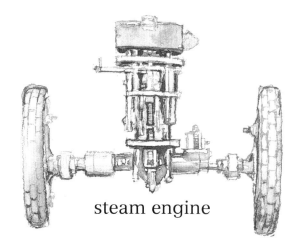

steam engine

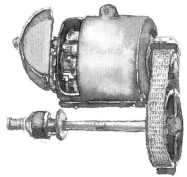

electric engine

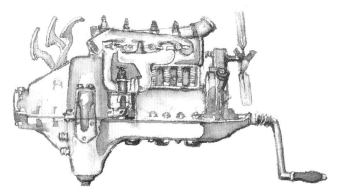

Model T engine